ISBN: 0-7172-8786-6

Manufactured in the United States of America.
A B C D   1 2 3 4

W9-BMR-168

Disney's POCAHONTAS

AND THE BABY EAGLE

GROLIER
BOOK CLUB EDITION

Summer was a busy time for the Powhatans. It was the season when the men of the village gathered the reeds that grew in the nearby river. While the women wove reed baskets, the men used the reeds to mend the village homes.

One day the women began to run out of
reeds. Since the men were busy patching
homes, Pocahontas offered to go to the river
and cut more reeds.

On her way to the river, Pocahontas saw
Meeko the raccoon stuffing himself with ripe
berries. Flit the hummingbird was there, too,
searching the wildflowers for nectar.

Pocahontas invited them to come with her to the river. Flit and Meeko were happy to go. Pocahontas always had wonderful stories to share with them.

Pocahontas told
her friends about the
time her father had
sat on a wasp.
"No one in the village had ever seen a man
jump so high," she said, "or yell so loudly!"

Meeko admired his reflection in the water. He wasn't afraid of tiny flying things like wasps!

Suddenly Flit zoomed down and gave Meeko a playful peck on his backside!

SPLASH! Meeko was so startled he fell headfirst into the river.

Pocahontas and Flit laughed as Meeko shook off the water. "We're all afraid of something, Meeko," Pocahontas said. "It seems you're afraid of hummingbirds!"

When Pocahontas had cut as many reeds
as she could carry, she said good-bye to her
friends. "I'll be back for more reeds soon,"
she called. "By then you should be nice
and dry, Meeko."

As Pocahontas started back to the village,
she noticed a large bird in the sky.

"Look at that eagle circling over us,"
she said. "He is making sure no
harm comes to his nest."

After Pocahontas left, Flit
buzzed around his raccoon friend,
hoping to play another game.
But Meeko just shook his paw at Flit.
He was still upset at the hummingbird for
playing a trick on him.

Suddenly something
hit Meeko on the head
with a heavy thump.
The raccoon thought
Flit was playing
another silly game.

But while Meeko rubbed his head, Flit
stared in amazement. On the ground in front
of him sat a baby eagle, crying!

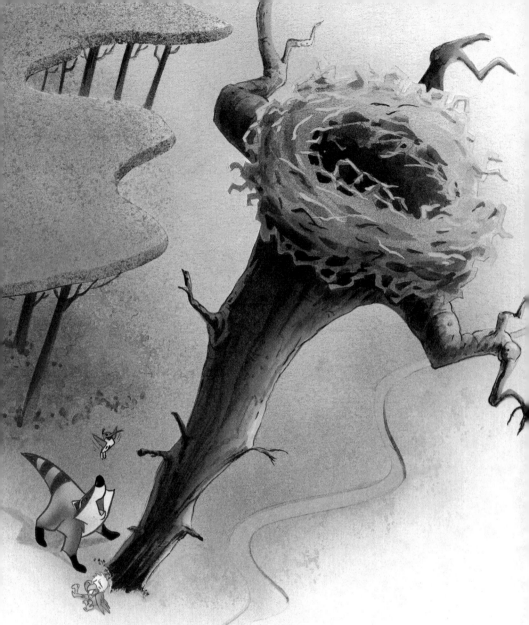

Flit and Meeko looked up. There, at the top of a tall tree, was the eagle's nest. They realized the baby bird must have fallen out of the nest. Luckily, he had landed on something soft—Meeko's head!

The little bird was not happy to find himself on the ground instead of in his nest. Meeko and Flit wondered what to do. Then Flit had an idea.

Flapping his wings as hard as he could, Flit
tried to carry the baby eagle back to his nest.

But the baby bird was
more than twice as big as
tiny Flit! The hummingbird could barely
lift the eagle off the ground.

Meeko chuckled. This was the silliest
thing he had ever seen.

The baby eagle didn't appreciate being
laughed at, so he nipped Meeko on the nose!

Then it was Flit's turn to laugh as
Meeko jumped behind the tree to get
away from the little bird.

It wasn't long before the baby eagle began
to cry again. While Meeko watched helplessly,
Flit darted away.

Seconds later the hummingbird returned
with some juicy berries. The little eagle
stopped crying for a moment, sniffed at the
berries, and turned away.

Meeko thought that Flit was
being silly again. Eagles didn't
eat berries. Eagles ate fish!
So Meeko headed toward
the river to catch a fish.

Normally Meeko was very good at finding
food. But catching a fish wasn't easy. As the
raccoon grabbed a fish from the water, he
slipped. SPLASH!

Just then Pocahontas returned for more reeds. She laughed. "I know that raccoons enjoy washing themselves, but two baths in one day, Meeko?"

If Meeko had been able to talk, he would have explained why he was in the water again.

Instead, Meeko led Pocahontas to the
baby eagle.

When Pocahontas saw the unfortunate
creature, she understood at once. "Oh, you
poor little thing! You've fallen out of your
nest," she said gently. "Don't worry, brave
eagle, I'll get you home."

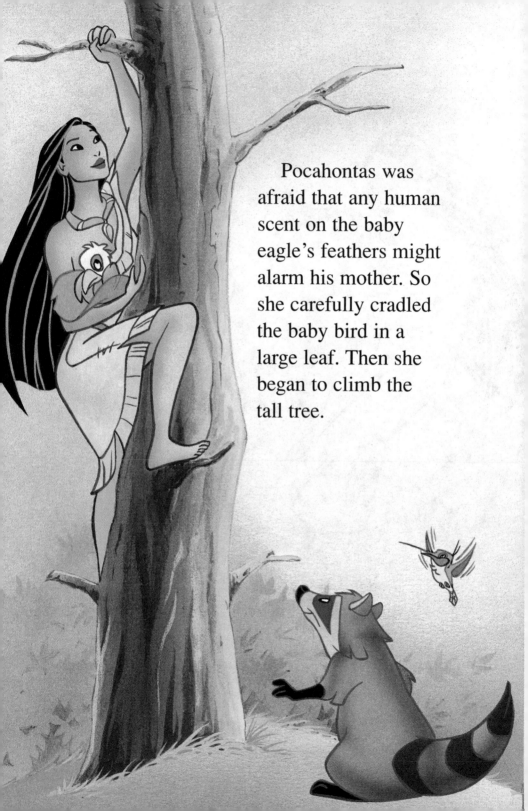

Pocahontas was afraid that any human scent on the baby eagle's feathers might alarm his mother. So she carefully cradled the baby bird in a large leaf. Then she began to climb the tall tree.

Suddenly a shadow fell across the tree.
Pocahontas heard an angry screech and
felt something rush at her. She twisted
away just in time to avoid the eagle's
sharp talons.

The father eagle was trying to protect his
nest. He didn't know that Pocahontas was
only trying to help. He whirled around the
tree, trying to chase the girl away.

Pocahontas jumped to the ground. She
couldn't risk being attacked again and falling
with the baby eagle.

"How can I climb up the tree?" she wondered. "I'm afraid the eagle might hurt me or his baby."

Then the clever girl had an idea. "You and Flit stay with the baby eagle," she told Meeko. "I'll be right back."

Pocahontas rushed back to the village and searched for a large basket. When she found the right one, she painted a special design on it. "This will do nicely," she said when she had finished.

Pocahontas returned with the basket on her back. Meeko and Flit didn't think a basket would protect her from the strong eagle.

But Pocahontas picked up the little eagle and began to climb the tree. Sure enough, the great eagle flew at her again, his talons flashing. But when he caught sight of the basket, he screeched in fear and flew away. Pocahontas was able to reach the top of the tree!

Pocahontas gently put the baby bird back
in his nest. "You'll be safe now," she said
with a smile. The baby eagle blinked and
gave a grateful chirp in return.

By the time Pocahontas reached the ground, the mother eagle had returned with a fish for her fledgling. She had no idea that her baby had been the cause of such great excitement.

The mother eagle fed her hungry baby.
After he finished his meal, the baby eagle
snuggled close to his mother, content in her
soft feathers.

Meeko smiled as he watched the baby's
reunion with his mother.
But when he saw what
Pocahontas had painted
on the basket, his smile
turned to shock!

Pocahontas laughed at her friend. "You see, Meeko, everyone's afraid of something. The eagle was afraid of the mountain lion face."

Still laughing, Pocahontas waved good-bye, saying, "And if I don't hurry home, I'm *afraid* I'll be late for supper!"